THE
Moon's Revenge

THE
Moon's Revenge

by JOAN AIKEN · illustrated by ALAN LEE

ALFRED A. KNOPF · NEW YORK

37521

THIS IS A BORZOI BOOK PUBLISHED BY ALFRED A. KNOPF, INC.

Text copyright © 1987 by Joan Aiken Enterprises Ltd.
Illustrations copyright © 1987 by Alan Lee.
All rights reserved under International and Pan-American Copyright Conventions.
Published in the United States by Alfred A. Knopf, Inc., New York. Distributed by
Random House, Inc., New York. Originally published in Great Britain by Jonathan
Cape Ltd., London. Manufactured in Great Britain
10   8   6   4   2   1   3   5   7   9

Library of Congress Cataloging-in-Publication Data
Aiken, Joan, 1924—   . The moon's revenge.
Summary: Seppy forces the moon to give him his wish, to be the maker of
enchanted fiddle music, but almost pays a horrible price for it.   [1. Musicians—
Fiction.   2. Moon—Fiction.   3. Wishes—Fiction]   I. Lee, Alan, ill.   II. Title.
PZ7.A2695Mn   1987   [Fic]   87-2863
ISBN 0-394-89380-8   ISBN 0-394-99380-2 (lib. bdg.)

ONCE THERE WAS A BOY CALLED SEPPY, and he was the seventh son of a seventh son. This was long ago, in the days when women wore shawls and men wore hoods and long pointed shoes, and the cure for an earache was to put a hot roasted onion in your ear.

Seppy's father was a coach maker. He made carts and carriages for all the farmers and gentry nearby. At the age of seven, Seppy had learned how to cut a panel for a carriage door and shave a spoke for a cartwheel. But what he *really* wanted was to play the fiddle. He had made himself a little one from odds and ends of wood in the yard. Sep's grandfather, people said, had been the best fiddler in the country. He had played so beautifully that two kings, King Henry and King Richard, had stopped fighting a great battle to listen, and the tears ran like rain down their faces until he finished playing and went on his way; then they picked up their swords and finished the battle.

"If it had been me," thought Sep, "I'd not have stopped playing. I'd have made those kings listen till they promised never to fight another battle."

Sep's father said he must learn the coach maker's trade.

"Put the fiddle away," he said. "That's for Sundays and holidays. You've got to earn your living."

There was an empty, ruined house in the little seaport where Sep lived. Nobody would stay in the house, because you could hear voices talking inside, even when it was empty. People said they must be the voices of devils.

"They might just as well be angels," thought Sep, and he climbed out of his bedroom window one frosty midnight and slipped along the dark cobbled street and stood, with his heart going pitapat, outside the broken door, listening.

He put his ear to a crack. Yes! He could hear voices, talking in quiet tones. What were they talking about? Afterward Sep could never remember.

But with his heart thumping even louder he tapped, and called in a whisper through the hole.

"Hey! You in there! If you please! How can I learn to be the best fiddler in the country?"

He laid his ear to the crack. A cold breeze blew out of it so sharply that Sep jumped back in fright.

"Throw your shoe at the moon," whispered a voice. "Each night for seven nights, throw your shoe at the moon."

"B-b-b-but *how*?" stammered Sep. "What shoe?"

Nobody answered. He could hear the voices talking again, to each other, not to him.

Sep tiptoed back to bed, scratching his head. He had only one pair of shoes, hogskin clogs in which he clattered about the coach yard. But when his feet were smaller he had worn other shoes, some passed on by his six elder brothers. His mother, who never wasted anything, kept all these little old pairs in a bag inside the grandfather clock.

So the next day, when his mother was out feeding the ducks and geese who swam in the river by the coach yard, Sep went quietly and found the bag. He took a pair of tiny, soft kidskin shoes that he had worn when he was one year old. And on a night when the moon was nearly full, he went down to the beach. He laid one of the shoes on the sea wall, looked at the cold, shiny sea and the black, wrinkled waves; then, with all his energy, he hurled the other little white shoe up—straight up—into the face of the white, watching moon.

What happened to the shoe? Sep couldn't see. It certainly didn't fall down onto the sand or into the sea; he was sure of that. He left the other shoe lying on the sea wall and went home to bed.

The next night he went to the beach again, and this time he threw up the small rabbitskin boot he had worn when he was two. Right into the face of the blazing moon. As before, he heard no sound of it falling back to the ground. And, leaving the other boot on the sea wall, he went home to bed.

On the third night, he threw up a red crocodile-skin slipper that a lord's wife had given his mother. Sep had worn them when he was three, and they were his favorite shoes, but he soon outgrew them. Straight into the face of the shining moon he threw the red shoe, and he left its mate lying on the sea wall.

On the fourth night he threw up a doeskin boot that a traveling musician had given his mother in exchange for a plate of stew. Sep had loved those boots, which were very light and comfortable; he had worn them when he was four. Into the face of the moon he tossed the boot. And he left the other boot on the sea wall.

On the fifth night he flung up a shiny calfskin shoe with a pewter buckle that all his brothers had worn in turn before him. And he left the other buckled shoe on the sea wall.

On the sixth night he threw up a sheepskin slipper that one of his six uncles had made for him when he was ill with measles at the age of six. And he left the other slipper on the sea wall.

On the seventh night he threw up one of his two hogskin clogs that he wore every day.

"One's no use without the other," thought Sep. He left the other clog on the sea wall. Now there were seven shoes in a row.

"People will think that a seven-footed monster has gone in swimming," thought Sep.

He looked up at the moon and blinked in fright. For the moon was blazing down at him with a face of fury. Its whiteness was all dirtied over with marks where he had thrown his shoes. And he could feel its anger scorching him, like the breath of an ice-dragon.

Sep turned and ran home as fast as he could on his bare feet, leaving the row of seven shoes on the wall casting long shadows in the moon's blaze of rage. But as he ran a thick white sea fog slid in over the beach; the shoes, the shadows, and the moon all vanished from view.

"I hope the moon isn't coming after me," thought Sep. He felt a prickle between his shoulders at the thought of the moon rolling after him, like a great wheel, through the fog.

Back home, he scurried up to his little attic bedroom, and jumped into bed, and hid under the covers. He soon fell asleep, but in the middle of the night he woke again, for now his room was full of moon, absolutely brimful of moon, like a goldfish bowl full of water.

Sep gasped with fright. But then he remembered that he was the seventh son of a seventh son, and he sat up boldly in bed.

"You must give me a wish," he told the moon. "It's the rule. They said so."

The moon's reply came in a freezing trickle of notes, like a peal of ice-bells, which made Sep's ears tingle all the way down to his stomach.

"Yes! I have to give you a wish, you impertinent boy! But you have marked my face forever with your dirty shoes, and for that I shall punish you. You must go barefoot for seven years. And until the day when you put those shoes back in the clock, your sister will not speak. And you and all your family will be in great danger—but I shan't tell you what it's going to be. You can just wait and see!"

With that, the moon sucked itself backward out of Sep's room, like a cloud through a keyhole, leaving the boy cold and scared and puzzled.

"Sister? I haven't got a sister," he thought. "What did the moon mean? And what can the danger be? I wish I knew. But at least I can get those shoes that I left on the sea wall, and put them back in the clock. Perhaps that will help."

The next morning, before sunrise, Sep ran down to the beach. From a long way off he could see the seven shoes on the wall, throwing long shadows as the sun slipped up out of the silver water. But just before Sep got there, a huge wave came rolling—green and black and blue, curved like a claw, rolling from far over the sea's rim—snatched up the seven shoes in its foaming lip, and carried them away, back over the rim of the sea.

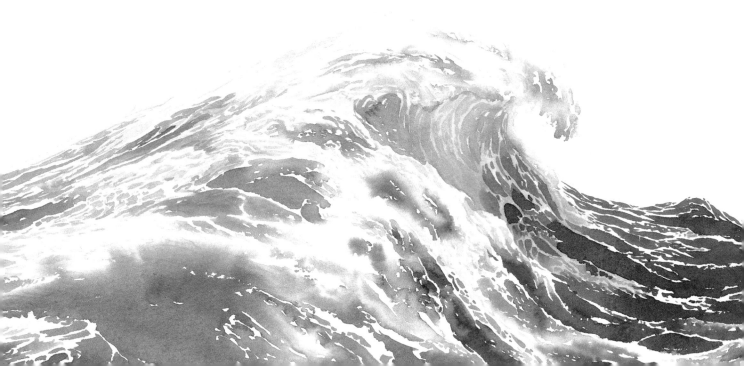

"Bother it!" said Sep, greatly annoyed and disappointed, and he walked home slowly, feeling the path cold and gritty under his bare feet.

Back at home, he found the family all excited, his father and brothers bustling about with hot water and wine and towels and milk, for a new baby had just been born to Sep's mother, a little girl called Octavia, with gray eyes and silvery pale hair. Everybody was so pleased, Sep didn't get much of a scolding for losing his shoes.

"But," said his father, "you'll go barefoot till you make yourself another pair."

Which was what Sep could *not* do: no shoes he made would stay on his feet more than half an hour. They cracked or split, the soles fell off, the laces broke, the canvas tore, the leather crumbled to powder. Sep's feet grew hard as horn and, except in the snowy winter, he did not mind this result of the moon's anger. The really unfair punishment had fallen on his little sister Octavia. When Sep looked at her he felt sadness like a skin of ice around his heart, for, though pretty as a peach and good as gold, she never learned to speak or sing, she never cried, she never made a single sound. She was dumb.

The years began to roll past, ticked away by the grandfather clock. Each evening Sep slipped away to the loft of one of his uncles, who was a sailmaker, and there he played his fiddle where no one could hear him—no one except the gulls and swallows who flew around the roof, and the mice who lived under the floorboards. As Sep taught himself to play better and better, they all stopped their flying and chewing, their pecking and scratching and munching, in order to listen, and remained stone-still all the time he played.

And little Octavia loved his playing best of all. As soon as she could
crawl and scramble and walk, she followed Sep everywhere and sat for
hours sucking her thumb while he played his tunes.

When there was a holiday, Sep carried her into the fields, or the
woods, or up on the moors, or for miles along the rocky beach, and
played his music where nobody listened but the rabbits, or the wild deer,
or the seals splashing in the foam. And everywhere he went the moon
followed, watching him with its cold eye.

When Octavia was a year old, beginning to walk, Sep's mother looked in the clock for the bag of shoes.

"That's queer," she said. "I could have sworn I left the bag in here—"

Sep was about to speak when his father said, "No, Meg, don't you remember? You gave the shoes to the clock mender—that time when the clock stopped and he set it going again?"

And to Sep's utter astonishment she answered, "Oh, yes, so I did, I gave them to the old man. And the clock has kept perfect time ever since."

Ticktock, ticktock, the clock went on keeping perfect time. Sep made Octavia shoes from sail canvas, with stitched rope soles. And she still followed him wherever he went.

One autumn day when she was three, Sep carried her on his shoulders along the shore. A great ship had been wrecked in a gale, far out to sea, and pieces of gilded wood, fine silks and velvets, colored wax candles, glass jars, and ivory boxes came floating and tossing ashore.

Sep was looking for a piece of wood. His little fiddle was no longer big enough, and he wanted a piece of rare maple, or royal pine, or seasoned sycamore—woods which were not to be found in his father's yard—so that he could make himself a new fiddle.

While he hunted along the water's edge, little Octavia skipped along at the foot of the cliff, picking up here a pebble or a shell, there a brooch or a pin that the waves had flung ashore.

Sep was tugging at the brass handle of a chest all wrapped in green weed when she ran up and jerked at his arm, beckoning him to come and pointing with her other hand.

What was she pointing at? Sep stared, and stared again. The thing at the cliff foot that he had at first taken for a gray rock was in fact a huge shoe—covered with barnacles and half-filled with pebbles—but *whose* shoe could it possibly be? Large as a fishing smack, it lay sunk in the sand. Little Octavia was dying to climb on it, but Sep would not let her. Suppose the shoe's owner came looking for it?

"Come away!" he said. "Come away, Octavia!"

The wind blew chilly, and a sea mist was rising. Sep felt a queer pitapat of the heart, as he had once before when he listened outside the empty house. He took his fiddle from his knapsack and played a tune— a frisking, laughing tune, to keep bad luck away. As he played, the mist grew thicker, and Sep was almost sure that he could see the ghost of a king in his robes at the water's edge. And was there not, also, the ghost of a ship, far out to sea, waiting for its master? The king nodded at Sep as if he were listening hard to the music—and liking it, too—then pointed his finger at the great gray shoe. As he pointed there came a rumbling—a louder rumbling—then a tremendous roaring crash—and half the cliff fell down, burying the shoe under a mountain of rock. If Sep and Octavia had been beside the shoe, they would have been buried as well.

A smaller rock, bouncing down the beach, split open the chest which Sep had been trying to drag free. Inside the chest was a canvas bag, waxed, and tied with cords. Inside that was another bag. Inside that was a leather case. And inside *that* was a beautiful violin, which had been so carefully packed that not one drop of sea water had touched it.

Sep carefully lifted out the violin, holding it as if it were made of gold.

Then he turned to where the ghost had stood by the water's edge—but nobody was there, not even a footprint.

"Did you see him?" Sep asked Octavia. But she shook her head.

Sep walked home with the new violin under his arm and Octavia riding on his back.

That evening he set the old violin on a plank, with a lighted candle stuck beside it, and let it float away, out to sea.

Ticktock, ticktock, the grandfather clock went on keeping perfect time until little Octavia was nearly seven, could sew and spin, could make butter and cakes and bread. She was good and pretty and cheerful, but still she never said a word.

Sep went on practicing his music as often and as long as he could. "Perhaps someday," he thought, "the music will teach Octavia how to speak." For in the meantime the music had saved them from some tight corners and helped them in several difficulties: when the smith's mastiff turned savage and ran at Octavia, when Sep's mother's blackberry jam would have boiled all over the kitchen if Sep's music hadn't calmed it down, and—worst of all—when the grandfather clock suddenly stopped ticking. Quick as a flash Sep, who happened to be beside it, snatched up his fiddle and played a rattling-quick tune, and the clock hummed, hawed, cleared its throat, and was off again, ticking as hard as ever.

One Sunday evening after church, all the village people were down on the slipway, chatting as they always did.

"A magpie has sat on the steeple for three days," someone said. "That means trouble."

"And there was a big red ring round the moon last night."

"And the bush in the churchyard has three black roses on it."

"Something dreadful must be going to happen," they all agreed.

"It's getting very dark," said Sep's father. "Look at that big black cloud."

The moon had risen, large, pale, and scowling, but a solid black cloud began to spread wider and wider across the sky, until it swallowed the moon in a pool of inky dark. For a moment a thin layer of light lay between black cloud and black sea; then something odd and bulky crossed the line of light.

"What was *that?*" said one of Sep's uncles. "Looked like a horned whale—"

"Maybe it was a boat," said somebody else.

"Daft kind of a boat—with horns!"

"There it goes again."

"It's coming closer!"

Now everybody could see something—some great Thing—coming in out of the sea, toward the land.

It moved so fast that it seemed to double in size as it came along.

"Oh! Oh! It's a dreadful beast!" screamed little Octavia. "Hide me, hide me, brother Seppy! It's coming this way. It's going to eat us all!"

The crowd scattered, screaming and terrified. For the monster churning toward them through inky waves had two great horns on its forehead and a jawful of teeth as long as doorposts; it had spines or prickles or plates of shell on its back and sides; and it had seven great feet at the end of seven great legs, which stomped and splashed through the water. As the creature came closer the townspeople caught a whiff of its smell, a damp, rotting, sickly, weedy breath, like water that flowers have been in for far too long. When it reached the end of the harbor bar, the beast stood still on its seven legs and let out a loud, threatening cry, like a sea lion that has swallowed a copper trumpet.

"It's hungry. We're all done for," gasped Sep's aunt Lucy. "That beast will swallow the lot of us, like a spoonful of peas."

"Please, brother Sep," squeaked little Octavia, "play it a tune on your fiddle. Pray, pray, play it a tune. You stopped the charging bull and the mad dog—perhaps you can stop this beast!"

All in the midst of his fright and horror, Sep suddenly noticed something.

"Octavia! You spoke! You said words!"

"Oh, never mind that, brother Sep! Fetch your fiddle!"

Still carrying Octavia, Sep hurried through the crowd to his uncle's sail loft, where he kept his fiddle hidden. A stair led up from the harbor front to an outside door. Sep stood on this stair and played his fiddle.

At first no one heard him. The crowd were yelling in terror, and the monster was booming most balefully. Then one or two people noticed Sep and began to jeer.

"What does the fool think he's doing?"

"Clodpole!"

"Loony!"

"Coward! You think it can't reach you up there?"

But as Sep calmly went on playing, the monster stopped its wailing and began to listen. Or so it seemed. The seven jerking, stamping legs stood still. The horned head slowly turned in the direction of Sep's music. Then the head began to nod up and down in time with the tune Sep was playing—which was a very lively tune, a sailors' hornpipe.

Then the monster began to dance.

Stomp, stomp went its legs again, but now they kicked high and gaily out of the water. The monster jigged and joggled, nodding its head, flapping all its prickles and plates. As the great scaly feet came up splashing out of the waves, it could be seen that they wore shoes. On one foot was a huge clog. On another, a laced boot. On another, a red slipper. On another, a black shoe with a buckle.

"If those are my shoes," thought Sep, astonished, playing away for dear life, "if those are my shoes, they have certainly grown."

"Don't stop playing, brother Sep!" squeaked little Octavia, jumping up and down in time to the tune. "The monster simply loves your music!"

"Don't stop, don't stop!" shouted all the people on the harbor front. "Don't stop for a single minute."

"Everybody play, who can!" shouted Sep, sawing away with his bow.

Anyone in the village who had a musical instrument ran home for it. They brought fiddles, drums, flutes, krummhorns, and tabors. They played and played. And the ones who had no instruments to play danced and sang. Sailors on ships far out to sea heard the sound and wondered what was going on. If Sep stopped playing for a moment, the monster noticed, through all the noise, that the sound of his fiddle was missing, and it began to cry.

"Don't stop, Sep!" everybody shouted. "You must keep on playing!"
It was like a frantic party that went on all night.

"How long *can* I go on?" Sep wondered. His arms ached so badly that
he wondered if they were going to fall off. Morning would soon be here;
the sky was growing pale.

"Don't stop, don't stop!" Octavia cried anxiously. Then she said,
"Look, Seppy! The monster is shrinking!"

Sep saw that this was true. Now the monster was no bigger than a
house. Now it was as small as a fishing boat. Now it was the size of a
cart. Now not even as large as a cow. Now, shrinking all the time, it
made a tremendous effort and sprang up onto the end of the pier. Then,
with an expiring squeak, it vanished altogether, whirling into the air
like a blown feather, just as the sun rose.

The townspeople were so tired that they flopped onto the cobbles where they stood, and fell asleep. But Sep, with little Octavia, ran down to the end of the pier, where they found seven odd shoes: a red slipper, a doeskin boot, a white kidskin shoe, a sheepskin slipper, a buckled shoe, a rabbitskin boot, and a hogskin clog.

Octavia helped Sep carry them home. "It's lucky we found them," she said, skipping along by him with her arms full of shoes. "We can put them in the bag in the clock, and all *my* children will be able to wear them when they are little."

"But there's only one of each pair," said Sep.

"No, there isn't! The others have been in that bag inside the clock ever since I can remember. I've played with them lots of times, pretending a seven-footed monster was wearing them."

Sure enough, Octavia pulled the bag out of the clock and put back the shoes. But she kept out the hogskin clogs and put them on. They fitted her feet exactly.

When the people on the quay woke up, they had forgotten all about the monster. Puzzled, scratching their heads, they wandered off homeward.

From that day, little Octavia could speak as well as anybody, and she did it twice as fast, to make up for lost time.

Sep went on working in his father's coach yard, but now, as well, he began to play his fiddle at weddings and feasts and parties. By and by he became famous all over the country—so famous that he was invited to play at all six weddings of King Henry VIII. And each time he played, the tears ran down King Henry's cheeks, and he said, "Oh, Sep, boy! I couldn't have played better myself."

For the king was a musician too.

Often, often, when Sep was walking homeward on a dark night, after playing his music at a wedding or a party, he would look up at the silvery face of the moon, with its black, dirty marks, and think: "Did I really put those marks there? Did I really do that dreadful thing to the poor moon? Or was it all a dream? I wish the moon would tell me!"

But the moon, scowling down at Sep, never spoke to him again.